To Sidhant and Antara, for being adventurous little travellers,
albeit the little matter of my having to carry milk cartons around the world.
—Natasha Sharma

Princess Easy Pleasy

Natasha Sharma

Priya Kuriyan

Princess Easy Pleasy was with her parents
in Hong Kong for their winter vacation.

Nothing was as she liked it to be.

'I will not drink this! I want the same milk I have at home,' protested Princess Easy Pleasy.

'Our perfect princess,' cooed the king and queen and called for the royal packer. 'Take note for our next vacation.'

So for their spring vacation to China along went the cow.

ROYAL PACKING LIST
1. Cow
2. Clothes
3.

'This tastes blah! I want my noodles
and vegetables just like I eat them at home!'
grumbled Princess Easy Pleasy.

'Our precious pudding,' fussed the king
and queen and turned to the royal packer.

So for their summer vacation to Singapore along went the chef.

'This feels hard! I want the mattress
to be bouncy like the one at home,'
demanded Princess Easy Pleasy.

'Our delicate darling,' fretted
the king and queen.

'A word, Royal Packer.'

So for their monsoon vacation to Cambodia
along went the bedding.

'This pony cannot prance like the one at home. The dogs are not as naughty. Even the rabbits are not as fluffy!' fussed Princess Easy Pleasy.

'Our playful pumpkin,'
worried the king and queen.

'Royal Packer . . . list.'

So for their autumn vacation to Thailand along went the pets.

'He is too tiny! I want the same one I ride at home!' complained Princess Easy Pleasy.

'Our impossible imp,'
panicked the king and queen.
'Royal Packer . . .'

So for their winter vacation to Sri Lanka . . .

'NO MORE VACATIONS!'

declared the queen.

Princess Easy Pleasy was bored.
Nothing was as she liked it to be.
She wanted to go on a vacation.

'On one condition . . .'
said the queen.

So, on Princess Easy Pleasy's vacation to Tibet,
she dressed like the locals, rode a yak, ate their food
and found that it was actually quite fun!

Text: Natasha Sharma
Illustrations: Priya Kuriyan

Karadi Tales Company Pvt. Ltd.
3A Dev Regency 11 First Main Road
Gandhinagar Adyar Chennai 600020
Ph: +91 44 4205 4243
Email: contact@karaditales.com
Website: www.karaditales.com

Printed in India
ISBN: 978-81-8190-335-8

Cataloging - in - Publication information:

Sharma, Natasha
Princess Easy Pleasy / Natasha Sharma ; illustrated by Priya Kuriyan
p.32; color illustrations ; 28 x 20.5 cm.

1. Travel--Juvenile literature. 2. Conduct of life--Humor.
3. Conduct of life--Juvenile fiction. 4. Selfishness--Juvenile fiction.

PZ7   [E]

JUV019000 JUVENILE FICTION / Humorous Stories
JUVENILE FICTION / Social Issues / Manners & Etiquette
JUV068000 JUVENILE FICTION / Travel

ISBN 978-81-8190-335-8

Printed in India
Distributed in the United States by Consortium Book Sales & Distribution
www.cbsd.com

Natasha Sharma is an award-winning children's book author with twelve books published till date.
Writing across age groups, from picture books to historical fiction for children under the History
Mystery series, she is extremely pleased to have found her way to the world of children's literature
with its sleepless nights of plotting and joyful moments of crazy character creation.

Priya Kuriyan is a children's book illustrator, comic book artist and an animator. A graduate of the
National Institute of Design (Ahmedabad), she has directed educational films for the Sesame Street
show (India) and the Children's Film Society of India (CFSI) and illustrated numerous children's
books for various Indian publishers. She currently lives in New Delhi, filling her sketchbooks with
funny caricatures of its residents.